Lydia of Philippi

Paul and his companions continued their travel, preaching the gospel wherever they went. They reached Philippi, a Roman colony, which was an important city in the district of Macedonia. They decided to stay there for some days.

On the Sabbath day or Sunday, they went out of the city to the riverside. They saw some women of the city who regularly met there for a prayer meeting. Paul and his friends joined them. Paul spoke to the women, explaining to them that if they believed in Jesus they could be saved from their sins.

A certain businesswoman named Lydia, who knew about Paul, came to the riverside to hear him. She was a seller of purple-dyed cloth from the city of Thyatira. High people in the society usually wore this expensive material. She worshipped God, but she really did not fully understand. As Paul preached,

the Lord opened her heart to believe what he said. She then accepted Jesus as Lord and was baptised along with the other members of her household.

Then, she invited Paul and the others to visit her home, which they joyfully did. So, Lydia was the first person to believe in Jesus in Philippi!

The Fortune Teller

It was Paul's custom to go along with his companions every day to pray. One day, a slave girl, possessed by a demon, met them. The girl was able to foretell certain things that could happen in the future, so her masters earned a lot of money through her fortune telling. This girl followed Paul and the others for many days and kept repeating, "These men are the servants of the Most High God!" Paul felt sorry for her.

One day, Paul angrily commanded the demon to come out of her and stop troubling her. The demon left her body at once. The girl could no longer tell the future. Her masters were furious when they realised that they could not earn money through her. Their whole business was lost!

Immediately, they caught Paul and Silas and dragged them to the marketplace before the authorities. They complained to them that

Paul and his fellow Jews were causing much trouble in the city. They were teaching the Roman people customs that were against their law to practice!

When they heard this, the people were very angry! The magistrates ordered the crowd to beat up Paul and his companions and imprison them.

Songs and Earthquakes

Paul and Silas were jailed. The jailer was instructed to carefully guard them. He, at once, thrust them into the inner prison and put their feet in chains.

However, Paul and Silas were not discouraged. At midnight, they were singing praises to God and praying. The other prisoners were

astonished to hear them!

Then something even more amazing happened. A great earthquake struck, shaking the prison to its very foundations! All the prison doors swung open! All the prisoners' chains fell off!

The horrified jailer woke up and saw the prison doors wide open! Thinking that the prisoners had escaped, he, at once, drew his sword to kill himself. But Paul quickly stopped him, saying, "Do not harm yourself, we are all here!"

The jailer immediately called for a light, and fell down trembling before Paul and Silas. Bringing them out, he asked, "Sirs, what must I do to be saved?"

They said, "Believe in Lord Jesus Christ, and you and your household will be saved."

When Paul preached, the jailer's entire household believed and was baptised. The jailer then washed their wounds, took them home and fed them, rejoicing in his new faith in Jesus!

Paul in Athens

Paul visited Athens. He was moved because of the great idolatry he saw. Paul then preached in the Temple and marketplace and to the religious people about Jesus, his death and resurrection. The Athenians did not understand. They wondered what foreign religion he was teaching. However, they loved to hear anything new!

Paul went to Mars Hill. Among the idols, he saw an altar built to 'the Unknown God!' Then Paul said he could see that though the Athenians were god-conscious they were ignorant about the true God. He told them how God created the world, and planned each person's life, when he would be born and where he would live. God made it possible that if man should seek Him, man can find Him. Paul said that earlier God had been patient when people had not sought Him, but now He commands all people everywhere to repent, because He has fixed a day when He will judge the world

in righteousness. Everyone will be raised after death because God raised Jesus from the dead.

When the Athenians heard about the resurrection, some mocked. But, others said, "We will hear you again about this." So, Paul went his way.

Paul in Corinth

Paul left Athens and went on to Corinth. There, he preached and reasoned in the synagogue every Sabbath, trying to persuade

the Jews and Greeks that belief in Jesus was the way to salvation.

When Silas and Timothy arrived from Macedonia, Paul was more encouraged to preach boldly. But his listeners actively opposed and mocked him. Paul angrily said, "You must bear the blame for rejecting Jesus!"

Paul then went to the house of a man named Justus, a worshiper of God. Justus' house was just next to the synagogue. Crispus, the chief ruler of the synagogue, believed and was baptised along with many Corinthians who believed.

One day, the Lord encouraged Paul in a vision, "Do not be afraid, but go on speaking and do not be silent, for I am with you, and no one will attack you to harm you, for I have many in this city who are my people."

Paul obediently stayed for a year and six months, effectively, teaching the Word of God among the Corinthians.

Paul and the Tent Makers

When Paul was in Corinth, he met Aquila and his wife Priscilla, a Jewish couple from Italy. Claudius, the Roman ruler, had commanded all the Jews to leave Rome, hence they had come here.

Paul was happy to know that the Jewish couple were tent makers. Though he was highly learned, Paul too, made tents to earn a living. Paul always believed in supporting himself. He was never a burden on anyone. So, Paul lived with Aquila and Priscilla and worked along with them.

Although Paul could have expected the Churches that he created, and the people to whom he preached, to support him in some way, yet he worked to provide for his own needs. Paul had always believed and encouraged his fellowmen to labour and toil, when they preached to the people about the Word of

God. That way neither Paul nor his disciples could be accused of laziness or dependence on others.

Aquila and Priscilla learnt much from Paul. They grew so close to him that they followed him on many missionary journeys. They supported Paul in his preaching work by teaching the young believers who visited their house. Paul loved them as his own family and when he was imprisoned, he wrote often, enquiring about them.

Aquila, Priscilla and Apollos

Paul travelled to Ephesus with Priscilla and Aquila. Then, he went on to Galatia to strengthen the believers in the growing Churches. Priscilla and Aquila stayed back in Ephesus.

At that time, a certain Jew named Apollos

visited Ephesus. He was widely read, and had studied the scriptures very well. He could speak very eloquently too. But he knew only about the baptism that John, the Baptist, had preached. He had not learnt that Jesus was the Saviour, the Promised One.

One day, he preached very passionately in the synagogue. Priscilla and Aquila were listening. They invited young Apollos home and taught him the Way of God more accurately. Apollos was a good and eager student. He quickly learnt all about Jesus and what he had taught, from Priscilla and Aquila. He was able to persuade the Jews more convincingly than before, because now he taught using the scriptures that Jesus was indeed the Messiah.

When Apollos decided to travel further and preach the gospel, the believers wrote letters encouraging the disciples there to receive him. When they did receive Apollos, he greatly helped in building up the new believers in the faith.

Sons of Sceva

God was working special and extraordinary miracles through Paul. Amazingly, even the handkerchiefs or aprons that had touched Paul's body had healing powers. When these were placed on the sick, they were immediately cured of their diseases, and evil spirits came out of those possessed by them!

Even, some of the travelling Jews began to cast out evil spirits, using Paul's name! They drove out devils saying, "We command you to come out in the name of Jesus, about whom Paul preaches."

One day, all the seven sons of Sceva, a Jewish high priest tried the same thing. But the evil spirit jumped on them, screaming, "Jesus I know, and Paul I recognise, but who are you?" Then the man with the evil spirit leaped on them, and overpowered them. They were so terrified that they literally ran out of the house, unclothed and wounded!

When the Jews and Greeks got to know of this happening, great fear fell upon them. Many who practised magic arts brought their books together and burnt them in front of everyone. Amazingly, the value of these books was fifty thousand pieces of silver!

Lord Jesus was greatly glorified and the Word of God triumphed!

The Riot of the Silversmiths

Paul remained in Asia for some time, dealing with several problems.

One day, Demetrius, a silversmith, who made shrines and idols of Goddess Diana, gathered the other craftsmen, saying, "Men, you know that we earn our money from this craft. But of late, not only in Ephesus but almost throughout

Asia, Paul has persuaded and turned the hearts of many, by preaching that Gods made with hands are not Gods. Soon both our trade and the Temple of our great Goddess Diana may be abandoned and nobody will worship her."

Hearing this, the city was filled with confusion. The enraged people shouted, "Great is Diana of the Ephesians!" They rushed to the public meeting place, dragging Paul's travel companions. Paul wanted to stop them, but he was restrained.

Alexander, the Jew, tried reasoning with the crowd, but for two whole hours they chanted, "Great is Diana of Ephesians!" Finally, the town clerk calmed the crowd by saying, "These men have neither robbed our Churches nor said anything bad about our Goddess. Therefore, if Demetrius and the craftsmen have any complaints, let them bring the charges to court. As it is, we have to answer for today's unnecessary riot." Then, he dismissed the assembly.

Boy Saved in Troas

On the first day of the week, that is the Lord's Day, the disciples gathered together in a room on the third floor of a building, to break bread, obeying Jesus' instructions. Paul was supposed to leave the next morning on another preaching journey.

So, Paul preached to them, reminding them how to live their lives, pleasing God. Paul kept talking and teaching for so long that it was midnight when he finished!

Among the people listening was a young man named Eutychus. He had been sitting at a window and fell into a deep sleep while Paul kept preaching. Suddenly, he fell from the window to the ground below!

Everybody was shocked! They thought that Eutychus had died. But Paul quickly went down and bent over him, and took him in his arms. Embracing him, Paul said, "Do not be alarmed, for he is not dead. He is alive."

Then they all came up again. They ate bread together and Paul continued talking with them for a little longer, until daybreak, and then he left.

They took young Eutychus away, alive and happy that nothing serious had happened.

Paul Says Goodbye

Paul decided to be in Jerusalem, if possible, on the Day of Pentecost. He sent for the elders of the Church of Ephesus to tell them for the last time, the Word of God and to wish

them goodbye. Once, he reached Jerusalem, he did not know what awaited him.

Paul reminded the elders how he had first come to them and taught them repentance towards God and faith in Jesus. He said that the Holy Spirit had told him of the suffering he still had to face, but he was not afraid. He simply wanted to finish his life here on Earth with joy.

Paul commended them to look after the young Churches, feeding the 'sheep' whom Jesus had saved by his own death on the cross. Paul told them to beware of 'wolves' that would harm the 'flock' as Paul himself had done with prayers and tears, for the past three years.

Finally, Paul advised them that it was more blessed to give than to receive! Then Paul knelt down, and prayed with them.

They all wept and kissed Paul, knowing they would never see him again. Then they escorted him to the ship and sadly waved him goodbye.

Paul in Jerusalem

In Caesarea, Paul stayed with Philip, the Evangelist. Agabus, a prophet, told Paul that he would be bound and imprisoned. The believers wept, advising Paul not to go to Jerusalem.

As Paul was unafraid, they sent him, saying, "The Lord's will be done."

One day, when he was in the Temple in Jerusalem, the Jews stirred up the people by saying, "This man has spread wrong teachings everywhere and has even brought the Greeks into the Temple to pollute it!"

The whole city was in uproar! Angrily, they dragged Paul out of the Temple and beat him, crying out to kill him. The chief captain brought Centurions to control the mob, and took Paul into the castle.

From the castle steps, Paul spoke in Hebrew to the Jews about how Jesus had encountered

him on the Damascus road. Paul was to bring the news of salvation to all men, whoever believed in Lord Jesus, including the Gentiles.

The mob now screamed, "Away with him!"

The captain ordered Paul to be scourged. Paul asked, "Can you lawfully scourge me, a free-born Roman citizen, without a trial?"

Quickly, the captain ordered Paul to be freed. Paul now had to face the Council.

Paul is Saved

After Paul faced the Council, they could not find any fault with him!

The Jews plotted to kill him. Forty Jews took an oath not to eat or drink till Paul was killed. When they told the chief priests their plan, Paul's sister's son heard it! Quickly, he went

to the castle where Paul was imprisoned and told him. Immediately, Paul told a Centurion, "Take this young man to the Tribune, Claudius Lysias, for he has something to tell him."

When the Tribune questioned him, the boy said, "The Jews swore to neither eat nor drink till they have killed Paul. They are ready, lying in wait for you to bring Paul before the Council again."

The Tribune, Lysias, called two Centurions and ordered two hundred soldiers, with seventy horsemen and two hundred spearmen, and a horse for Paul to ride, to take him safely to Felix, the Governor.

Then, Lysias wrote a letter to the Governor explaining that the Jews had seized Paul over some issue with Jewish law that was not worthy of death.

Felix read the letter. He commanded that Paul be kept in Herod's Judgement Hall until the Jews who accused him arrived too.

Paul in Caesarea

Felix waited for the Jewish leaders to come. After five days, the high priest Ananias and the Jewish elders arrived and presented their case against Paul. They said that Paul was the ringleader of the Nazarene sect and was causing confusion among the Jews the world over!

"You examine him and find out for yourself," they said.

The Governor asked Paul to defend himself.

Commending Felix for judging the people for many years, Paul said that just twelve days earlier, he had gone to worship in the Temple in Jerusalem. No one found any fault with him then nor did they see him creating any trouble in the synagogues or the city. Paul stated his belief in the Jewish law and also that Jesus fulfilled the law by his death and resurrection.

Felix, knowing the people very well, postponed giving his judgement until Lysias, the Tribune, also came.

Felix later sent for Paul. While reasoning with him about righteousness and self-control and God's coming judgement, Felix trembled in fear. Finally, Felix sent Paul away.

Two years later, Porcius Festus became Governor. To please the Jews, Felix still kept Paul imprisoned.

Paul Before Festus

After Festus became Governor, he went to Jerusalem. The high priest and Jewish leaders there informed him about Paul. They asked him to send for him. They thought that they could kill Paul as he travelled on his way to Jerusalem.

But Festus refused. He said he would return to Caesarea, and that the Jewish elders who

wished to accuse Paul were to accompany him!

After ten days, Festus returned. The next day, he summoned Paul before the judgement seat.

The Jews from Jerusalem accused Paul of doing terrible things, but unfortunately they could not prove anything!

Paul replied that he had done nothing wrong against the Jewish law, Temple or even Caesar, and even Festus knew that!

Festus, trying to please the Jews, asked Paul if he would consent to go to Jerusalem and answer before the Jews there.

Paul said that he was willing to die if he had done anything worthy of death. But since he had offended neither the Jewish law nor the Roman law, and no one could prove his guilt, he would like to appeal to Caesar.

Festus then consulted the Council and said, "Paul, to Caesar you have appealed and to Caesar you shall go!"

Also available in the **15 Stories** series

Aesop's Fables (Set of 48 books)